Leonard Kebler, John Greenleaf Whittier

Among the Hills

And other Poems

Leonard Kebler, John Greenleaf Whittier

Among the Hills
And other Poems

ISBN/EAN: 9783337327415

Printed in Europe, USA, Canada, Australia, Japan

Cover: Foto ©Andreas Hilbeck / pixelio.de

More available books at **www.hansebooks.com**

AND

OTHER POEMS.

BY

.

JOHN GREENLEAF WHITTIER.

BOSTON:

FIELDS, OSGOOD, & CO.,

SUCCESSORS TO TICKNOR AND FIELDS.

1869.

TO

ANNIE FIELDS,

𝔗𝔥𝔦𝔰 𝔏𝔦𝔱𝔱𝔩𝔢 𝔙𝔬𝔩𝔲𝔪𝔢,

DESCRIPTIVE OF SCENES WITH WHICH SHE IS FAMILIAR,

IS

GRATEFULLY OFFERED.

CONTENTS.

AMONG THE HILLS.

1*

PRELUDE.

A LONG the roadside, like the flowers of gold
    That tawny Incas for their gardens wrought,
Heavy with sunshine droops the golden-rod,
And the red pennons of the cardinal-flowers
Hang motionless upon their upright staves.
The sky is hot and hazy, and the wind,
Wing-weary with its long flight from the south,
Unfelt ; yet, closely scanned, yon maple leaf
With faintest motion, as one stirs in dreams,

Who clothes with grace all duty ; still, I know

Too well the picture has another side, —

How wearily the grind of toil goes on

Where love is wanting, how the eye and ear

And heart are starved amidst the plenitude

Of nature, and how hard and colorless

Is life without an atmosphere. I look

Across the lapse of half a century,

And call to mind old homesteads, where no flower

Told that the spring had come, but evil weeds,

Nightshade and rough-leaved burdock in the place

Of the sweet doorway greeting of the rose

And honeysuckle, where the house walls seemed

Blistering in sun, without a tree or vine

To cast the tremulous shadow of its leaves

Across the curtainless windows from whose panes

Fluttered the signal rags of shiftlessness ;

Within, the cluttered kitchen-floor, unwashed

(Broom-clean I think they called it) ; the best
    room

Stifling with cellar damp, shut from the air

In hot midsummer, bookless, pictureless

Save the inevitable sampler hung

Over the fireplace, or a mourning-piece,

A green-haired woman, peony-cheeked, beneath

Impossible willows ; the wide-throated hearth

Bristling with faded pine-boughs half concealing

The piled-up rubbish at the chimney's back ;

And, in sad keeping with all things about them,

Shrill, querulous women, sour and sullen men,

Untidy, loveless, old before their time,

With scarce a human interest save their own

Monotonous round of small economies,

Or the poor scandal of the neighborhood ;

Blind to the beauty everywhere revealed,

Treading the May-flowers with regardless feet ;

For them the song-sparrow and the bobolink

Sang not, nor winds made music in the leaves ;

For them in vain October's holocaust

Burned, gold and crimson, over all the hills,

The sacramental mystery of the woods.

Church-goers, fearful of the unseen Powers,

But grumbling over pulpit-tax and pew-rent,

Saving, as shrewd economists, their souls

And winter pork with the least possible outlay

Of salt and sanctity ; in daily life

Showing as little actual comprehension

Of Christian charity and love and duty,

As if the Sermon on the Mount had been

Outdated like a last year's almanac :

Rich in broad woodlands and in half-tilled fields,

And yet so pinched and bare and comfortless,

The veriest straggler limping on his rounds,

The sun and air his sole inheritance,

Laughed at a poverty that paid its taxes,

And hugged his rags in self-complacency!

Not such should be the homesteads of a land

Where whoso wisely wills and acts may dwell

As king and lawgiver, in broad-acred state,

With beauty, art, taste, culture, books, to make

His hour of leisure richer than a life

Of fourscore to the barons of old time,

Our yeoman should be equal to his home

Set in the fair, green valleys, purple walled,

A man to match his mountains, not to creep

Dwarfed and abased below them. I would fain

In this light way (of which I needs must own

With the knife-grinder of whom Canning sings,

"Story, God bless you! I have none to tell you!")

Invite the eye to see and heart to feel

The beauty and the joy within their reach, —

Home, and home loves, and the beatitudes

Of nature free to all.   Haply in years

That wait to take the places of our own,

Heard where some breezy balcony looks down

On happy homes, or where the lake in the moon

Sleeps dreaming of the mountains, fair as Ruth,

In the old Hebrew pastoral, at the feet

Of Boaz, even this simple lay of mine

May seem the burden of a prophecy,

Finding its late fulfilment in a change

Slow as the oak's growth, lifting manhood up

Through broader culture, finer manners, love,

And reverence, to the level of the hills.

O Golden Age, whose light is of the dawn,

And not of sunset, forward, not behind,

Flood the new heavens and earth, and with thee

    bring

All the old virtues, whatsoever things

Are pure and honest and of good repute,

But add thereto whatever bard has sung

Or seer has told of when in trance and dream

They saw the Happy Isles of prophecy !

Let Justice hold her scale, and Truth divide

Between the right and wrong ; but give the heart

The freedom of its fair inheritance ;

Let the poor prisoner, cramped and starved so long,

At Nature's table feast his ear and eye

With joy and wonder ; let all harmonies

Of sound, form, color, motion, wait upon

The princely guest, whether in soft attire

Of leisure clad, or the coarse frock of toil.

And, lending life to the dead form of faith,

Give human nature reverence for the sake

Of One who bore it, making it divine

With the ineffable tenderness of God ;

Let common need, the brotherhood of prayer,

The heirship of an unknown destiny,

The unsolved mystery round about us, make

A man more precious than the gold of Ophir.

Sacred, inviolate, unto whom all things

Should minister, as outward types and signs

Of the eternal beauty which fulfils

The one great purpose of creation, Love,

The sole necessity of Earth and Heaven!

AMONG THE HILLS.

F OR weeks the clouds had raked the hills
    And vexed the vales with raining,
And all the woods were sad with mist,
    And all the brooks complaining.

At last, a sudden night-storm tore
    The mountain veils asunder,
And swept the valleys clean before
    The besom of the thunder.

Through Sandwich notch the west-wind sang
    Good morrow to the cotter ;
And once again Chocorua's horn
    Of shadow pierced the water.

Above his broad lake Ossipee,
　　Once more the sunshine wearing,
Stooped, tracing on that silver shield
　　His grim armorial bearing.

Clear drawn against the hard blue sky
　　The peaks had winter's keenness;
And, close on autumn's frost, the vales
　　Had more than June's fresh greenness.

Again the sodden forest floors
　　With golden lights were checkered,
Once more rejoicing leaves in wind
　　And sunshine danced and flickered.

It was as if the summer's late
　　Atoning for its sadness
Had borrowed every season's charm
　　To end its days in gladness.

I call to mind those banded vales

    Of shadow and of shining,

Through which, my hostess at my side,

    I drove in day's declining.

We held our sideling way above

    The river's whitening shallows,

By homesteads old, with wide-flung barns

    Swept through and through by swallows, —

By maple orchards, belts of pine

    And larches climbing darkly

The mountain slopes, and, over all,

    The great peaks rising starkly.

You should have seen that long hill-range

    With gaps of brightness riven, —

How through each pass and hollow streamed

    The purpling lights of heaven, —

Rivers of gold-mist flowing down
    From far celestial fountains, —
The great sun flaming through the rifts
    Beyond the wall of mountains!

We paused at last where home-bound cows
    Brought down the pasture's treasure,
And in the barn the rhythmic flails
    Beat out a harvest measure.

We heard the night-hawk's sullen plunge,
    The crow his tree-mates calling :
The shadows lengthening down the slopes
    About our feet were falling.

And through them smote the level sun
    In broken lines of splendor,
Touched the gray rocks and made the green
    Of the shorn grass more tender.

The maples bending o'er the gate,
  Their arch of leaves just tinted
With yellow warmth, the golden glow
  Of coming autumn hinted.

Keen white between the farm-house showed,
  And smiled on porch and trellis,
The fair democracy of flowers
  That equals cot and palace.

And weaving garlands for her dog,
  'Twixt chidings and caresses,
A human flower of childhood shook
  The sunshine from her tresses.

On either hand we saw the signs
  Of fancy and of shrewdness,
Where taste had wound its arms of vines
  Round thrift's uncomely rudeness.

2

The sun-brown farmer in his frock
Shook hands, and called to Mary :
Bare-armed, as Juno might, she came,
White-aproned from her dairy.

Her air, her smile, her motions, told
Of womanly completeness ;
A music as of household songs
Was in her voice of sweetness.

Not beautiful in curve and line,
But something more and better,
The secret charm eluding art,
Its spirit, not its letter ; —

An inborn grace that nothing lacked
Of culture or appliance, —
The warmth of genial courtesy,
The calm of self-reliance.

Before her queenly womanhood

    How dared our hostess utter

The paltry errand of her need

    To buy her fresh-churned butter ?

She led the way with housewife pride,

    Her goodly store disclosing,

Full tenderly the golden balls

    With practised hands disposing.

Then, while along the western hills

    We watched the changeful glory

Of sunset, on our homeward way,

    I heard her simple story.

The early crickets sang ; the stream

    Plashed through my friend's narration :

Her rustic patois of the hills

    Lost in my free translation.

"More wise," she said, "than those who swarm
    Our hills in middle summer,
She came, when June's first roses blow,
    To greet the early comer.

"From school and ball and rout she came,
    The city's fair, pale daughter,
To drink the wine of mountain air
    Beside the Bearcamp Water.

"Her step grew firmer on the hills
    That watch our homesteads over ;
On cheek and lip, from summer fields,
    She caught the bloom of clover.

"For health comes sparkling in the streams
    From cool Chocorua stealing :
There 's iron in our Northern winds ;
    Our pines are trees of healing.

"She sat beneath the broad-armed elms

    That skirt the mowing-meadow,

And watched the gentle west-wind weave

    The grass with shine and shadow.

"Beside her, from the summer heat

    To share her grateful screening,

With forehead bared, the farmer stood,

    Upon his pitchfork leaning.

"Framed in its damp, dark locks, his face

    Had nothing mean or common, —

Strong, manly, true, the tenderness

    And pride beloved of woman.

"She looked up, glowing with the health

    The country air had brought her,

And, laughing, said : ' You lack a wife,

    Your mother lacks a daughter.

" ' To mend your frock and bake your bread
    You do not need a lady :
Be sure among these brown old homes
    Is some one waiting ready, —

" ' Some fair, sweet girl with skilful hand
    And cheerful heart for treasure,
Who never played with ivory keys,
    Or danced the polka's measure.'

" He bent his black brows to a frown,
    He set his white teeth tightly.
' 'T is well,' he said, ' for one like you
    To choose for me so lightly.

" ' You think, because my life is rude,
    I take no note of sweetness :
I tell you love has naught to do
    With meetness or unmeetness.

" ' Itself its best excuse, it asks

No leave of pride or fashion

When silken zone or homespun frock

It stirs with throbs of passion. .

" ' You think me deaf and blind : you bring

Your winning graces hither

As free as if from cradle-time

We two had played together.

" ' You tempt me with your laughing eyes,

Your cheek of sundown's blushes,

A motion as of waving grain,

A music as of thrushes.

" ' The plaything of your summer sport,

The spells you weave around me

You cannot at your will undo,

Nor leave me as you found me.

" ' You go as lightly as you came,
   Your life is well without me ;
What care you that these hills will close
   Like prison-walls about me?

" ' No mood is mine to seek a wife,
   Or daughter for my mother :
Who loves you loses in that love
   All power to love another!

" ' I dare your pity or your scorn,
   With pride your own exceeding ;
I fling my heart into your lap
   Without a word of pleading.'

" She looked up in his face of pain
   So archly, yet so tender :
'And if I lend you mine,' she said,
   ' Will you forgive the lender?

"'Nor frock nor tan can hide the man ;
    And see you not, my farmer,
How weak and fond a woman waits
    Behind this silken armor?

"'I love you : on that love alone,
    And not my worth, presuming,
Will you not trust for summer fruit
    The tree in May-day blooming ?'

"Alone the hangbird overhead,
    His hair-swung cradle straining,
Looked down to see love's miracle, —
    The giving that is gaining.

"And so the farmer found a wife,
    His mother found a daughter :
There looks no happier home than hers
    On pleasant Bearcamp Water.

2*   c

"Flowers spring to blossom where she walks
 The careful ways of duty;
Our hard, stiff lines of life with her
 Are flowing curves of beauty.

"Our homes are cheerier for her sake,
 Our door-yards brighter blooming,
And all about the social air
 Is sweeter for her coming.

"Unspoken homilies of peace
 Her daily life is preaching;
The still refreshment of the dew
 Is her unconscious teaching.

"And never tenderer hand than hers
 Unknits the brow of ailing;
Her garments to the sick man's ear
 Have music in their trailing.

"And when, in pleasant harvest moons,

　The youthful huskers gather,

Or sleigh-drives on the mountain ways

　Defy the winter weather, —

"In sugar-camps, when south and warm

　The winds of March are blowing,

And sweetly from its thawing veins

　The maple's blood is flowing, —

"In summer, where some lilied pond

　Its virgin zone is baring,

Or where the ruddy autumn fire

　Lights up the apple-paring, —

"The coarseness of a ruder time

　Her finer mirth displaces,

A subtler sense of pleasure fills

　Each rustic sport she graces.

"Her presence lends its warmth and health
  To all who come before it.
If woman lost us Eden, such
  As she alone restore it.

"For larger life and wiser aims
  The farmer is her debtor;
Who holds to his another's heart
  Must needs be worse or better.

"Through her his civic service shows
  A purer-toned ambition;
No double consciousness divides
  The man and politician.

"In party's doubtful ways he trusts
  Her instincts to determine;
At the loud polls, the thought of her
  Recalls Christ's Mountain Sermon.

" He owns her logic of the heart,

   And wisdom of unreason,

Supplying, while he doubts and weighs,

   The needed word in season.

" He sees with pride her richer thought,

   Her fancy's freer ranges ;

And love thus deepened to respect

   Is proof against all changes.

" And if she walks at ease in ways

   His feet are slow to travel,

And if she reads with cultured eyes

   What his may scarce unravel,

" Still clearer, for her keener sight

   Of beauty and of wonder,

He learns the meaning of the hills

   He dwelt from childhood under.

"And higher, warmed with summer lights,
    Or winter-crowned and hoary,
The ridged horizon lifts for him
    Its inner veils of glory.

"He has his own free, bookless lore,
    The lessons nature taught him,
The wisdom which the woods and hills
    And toiling men have brought him:

"The steady force of will whereby
    Her flexile grace seems sweeter;
The sturdy counterpoise which makes
    Her woman's life completer:

"A latent fire of soul which lacks
    No breath of love to fan it;
And wit, that, like his native brooks,
    Plays over solid granite.

"How dwarfed against his manliness

 She sees the poor pretension,

The wants, the aims, the follies, born

 Of fashion and convention !

"How life behind its accidents

 Stands strong and self-sustaining,

The human fact transcending all

 The losing and the gaining.

"And so, in grateful interchange

 Of teacher and of hearer,

Their lives their true distinctness keep

 While daily drawing nearer.

"And if the husband or the wife

 In home's strong light discovers

Such slight defaults as failed to meet

 The blinded eyes of lovers,

"Why need we care to ask? — who dreams
    Without their thorns of roses,
Or wonders that the truest steel
    The readiest spark discloses?

"For still in mutual sufferance lies
    The secret of true living:
Love scarce is love that never knows
    The sweetness of forgiving.

"We send the Squire to General Court,
    He takes his young wife thither;
No prouder man election day
    Rides through the sweet June weather.

"He sees with eyes of manly trust
    All hearts to her inclining;
Not less for him his household light
    That others share its shining."

Thus, while my hostess spake, there grew
  Before me, warmer tinted
And outlined with a tenderer grace,
  The picture that she hinted.

The sunset smouldered as we drove
  Beneath the deep hill-shadows.
Below us wreaths of white fog walked
  Like ghosts the haunted meadows.

Sounding the summer night, the stars
  Dropped down their golden plummets;
The pale arc of the Northern lights
  Rose o'er the mountain summits, —

Until, at last, beneath its bridge,
  We heard the Bearcamp flowing,
And saw across the mapled lawn
  The welcome home-lights glowing; —

And, musing on the tale I heard,

　'T were well, thought I, if often

To rugged farm-life came the gift

　To harmonize and soften ; —

If more and more we found the troth

　Of fact and fancy plighted,

And culture's charm and labor's strength

　In rural homes united, —

The simple life, the homely hearth,

　With beauty's sphere surrounding,

And blessing toil where toil abounds

　With graces more abounding.

MISCELLANEOUS POEMS.

THE CLEAR VISION.

I DID but dream. I never knew
   What charms our sternest season wore.
Was never yet the sky so blue,
   Was never earth so white before.
Till now I never saw the glow
Of sunset on yon hills of snow,
And never learned the bough's designs
Of beauty in its leafless lines.

Did ever such a morning break
   As that my eastern windows see?
Did ever such a moonlight take
   Weird photographs of shrub and tree?

Rang ever bells so wild and fleet
The music of the winter street?
Was ever yet a sound by half
So merry as yon school-boy's laugh?

O Earth! with gladness overfraught,
    No added charm thy face hath found;
Within my heart the change is wrought,
    My footsteps make enchanted ground.
From couch of pain and curtained room
Forth to thy light and air I come,
To find in all that meets my eyes
The freshness of a glad surprise.

Fair seem these winter days, and soon
    Shall blow the warm west winds of spring
To set the unbound rills in tune,
    And hither urge the bluebird's wing.

The vales shall laugh in flowers, the woods

Grow misty green with leafing buds,

And violets and wind-flowers sway

Against the throbbing heart of May.

Break forth, my lips, in praise, and own

   The wiser love severely kind ;

Since, richer for its chastening grown,

   I see, whereas I once was blind.

The world, O Father ! hath not wronged

With loss the life by thee prolonged ;

But still, with every added year,

More beautiful thy works appear !

As thou hast made thy world without,

   Make thou more fair my world within ;

Shine through its lingering clouds of doubt ;

   Rebuke its haunting shapes of sin ;

Fill, brief or long, my granted span

Of life with love to thee and man ;

Strike when thou wilt the hour of rest,

But let my last days be my best!

2d Month, 1868.

THE DOLE OF JARL THORKELL.

THE land was pale with famine
  And racked with fever-pain ;
The frozen fiords were fishless,
  The earth withheld her grain.

Men saw the boding Fylgja
  Before them come and go,
And, through their dreams, the Urdar-moon
  From west to east sailed slow !

Jarl Thorkell of Thevera
  At Yule-time made his vow ;
On Rykdal's holy Doom-stone
  He slew to Frey his cow.

3   D

To bounteous Frey he slew her ;

   To Skuld, the younger Norn,

Who watches over birth and death,

   He gave her calf unborn.

And his little gold-haired daughter

   Took up the sprinkling-rod,

And smeared with blood the temple

   And the wide lips of the god.

Hoarse below, the winter water

   Ground its ice-blocks o'er and o'er ;

Jets of foam, like ghosts of dead waves,

   Rose and fell along the shore.

The red torch of the Jokul,

   Aloft in icy space,

Shone down on the bloody Horg-stones

   And the statue's carven face.

And closer round and grimmer
  Beneath its baleful light
The Jotun shapes of mountains
  Came crowding through the night.

The gray-haired Hersir trembled
  As a flame by wind is blown ;
A weird power moved his white lips,
  And their voice was not his own !

" The Æsir thirst !" he muttered ;
  " The gods must have more blood
Before the tun shall blossom
  Or fish shall fill the flood.

" The Æsir thirst and hunger,
  And hence our blight and ban ;
The mouths of the strong gods water
  For the flesh and blood of man !

"Whom shall we give the strong ones?

   Not warriors, sword on thigh;

But let the nursling infant

   And bedrid old man die."

"So be it!" cried the young men,

   "There needs nor doubt nor parle";

But, knitting hard his red brows,

   In silence stood the Jarl.

A sound of woman's weeping

   At the temple door was heard;

But the old men bowed their white heads,

   And answered not a word.

Then the Dream-wife of Thingvalla,

   A Vala young and fair,

Sang softly, stirring with her breath

   The veil of her loose hair.

She sang : " The winds from Alfheim

   Bring never sound of strife ;

The gifts for Frey the meetest

   Are not of death, but life.

" He loves the grass-green meadows,

   The grazing kine's sweet breath ;

He loathes your bloody Horg-stones,

   Your gifts that smell of death.

" No wrong by wrong is righted,

   No pain is cured by pain ;

The blood that smokes from Doom-rings

   Falls back in redder rain.

" The gods are what you make them,

   As earth shall Asgard prove ;

And hate will come of hating,

   And love will come of love.

" Make dole of skyr and black bread
　　That old and young may live ;
And look to Frey for favor
　　When first like Frey you give.

" Even now o'er Njord's sea-meadows
　　The summer dawn begins ;
The tun shall have its harvest,
　　The fiord its glancing fins."

Then up and swore Jarl Thorkell :
　　" By Gimli and by Hel,
O Vala of Thingvalla,
　　Thou singest wise and well !

" Too dear the Æsir's favors
　　Bought with our children's lives ;
Better die than shame in living
　　Our mothers and our wives.

" The full shall give his portion
　　To him who hath most need ;
Of curdled skyr and black bread,
　　Be daily dole decreed."

He broke from off his neck-chain
　　Three links of beaten gold ;
And each man, at his bidding,
　　Brought gifts for young and old.

Then mothers nursed their children,
　　And daughters fed their sires,
And Health sat down with Plenty
　　Before the next Yule fires.

The Horg-stones stand in Rykdal ;
　　The Doom-ring still remains ;
But the snows of a thousand winters
　　Have washed away the stains.

Christ ruleth now ; the Æsir

Have found their twilight dim ;

And, wiser than she dreamed, of old

The Vala sang of Him !

THE TWO RABBIS.

THE Rabbi Nathan, twoscore years and ten,

Walked blameless through the evil world, and

then,

Just as the almond blossomed in his hair,

Met a temptation all too strong to bear,

And miserably sinned. So, adding not

Falsehood to guilt, he left his seat, and taught

No more among the elders, but went out

From the great congregation girt about

With sackcloth, and with ashes on his head,

Making his gray locks grayer. Long he prayed,

Smiting his breast ; then, as the Book he laid

Open before him for the Bath-Col's choice,

Pausing to hear that Daughter of a Voice,

3*

Behold the royal preacher's words: " A friend

Loveth at all times, yea, unto the end ;

And for the evil day thy brother lives."

Marvelling, he said: " It is the Lord who gives

Counsel in need.   At Ecbatana dwells

Rabbi Ben Isaac, who all men excels

In righteousness and wisdom, as the trees

Of Lebanon the small weeds that the bees

Bow with their weight.   I will arise, and lay

My sins before him."

          And he went his way

Barefooted, fasting long, with many prayers ;

But even as one who, followed unawares,

Suddenly in the darkness feels a hand

Thrill with its touch his own, and his cheek fanned

By odors subtly sweet, and whispers near

Of words he loathes, yet cannot choose but hear,

So, while the Rabbi journeyed, chanting low

The wail of David's penitential woe,

Before him still the old temptation came,

And mocked him with the motion and the shame

Of such desires that, shuddering, he abhorred

Himself; and, crying mightily to the Lord

To free his soul and cast the demon out,

Smote with his staff the blankness round about.

At length, in the low light of a spent day,

The towers of Ecbatana far away

Rose on the desert's rim ; and Nathan, faint

And footsore, pausing where for some dead saint

The faith of Islam reared a doméd tomb,

Saw some one kneeling in the shadow, whom

He greeted kindly : " May the Holy One

Answer thy prayers, O stranger ! " Whereupon

The shape stood up with a loud cry, and then,

Clasped in each other's arms, the two gray men
Wept, praising Him whose gracious providence
Made their paths one.   But straightway, as the sense
Of his transgression smote him, Nathan tore
Himself away: "O friend beloved, no more
Worthy am I to touch thee, for I came,
Foul from my sins, to tell thee all my shame.
Haply thy prayers, since naught availeth mine,
May purge my soul, and make it white like thine.
Pity me, O Ben Isaac, I have sinned!"

Awestruck Ben Isaac stood.   The desert wind
Blew his long mantle backward, laying bare
The mournful secret of his shirt of hair.
"I too, O friend, if not in act," he said,
"In thought have verily sinned.   Hast thou not read,
'Better the eye should see than that desire
Should wander?'   Burning with a hidden fire

That tears and prayers quench not, I come to thee

For pity and for help, as thou to me.

Pray for me, O my friend!"   But Nathan cried,

" Pray thou for me, Ben Isaac! "

                                        Side by side

In the low sunshine by the turban stone

They knelt ; each made his brother's woe his own,

Forgetting, in the agony and stress

Of pitying love, his claim of selfishness ;

Peace, for his friend besought, his own became ;

His prayers were answered in another's name ;

And, when at last they rose up to embrace,

Each saw God's pardon in his brother's face !

Long after, when his headstone gathered moss,

Traced on the targum-marge of Onkelos

In Rabbi Nathan's hand these words were read :

" Hope not the cure of sin till Self is dead;

Forget it in love's service, and the debt

Thou canst not pay the angels shall forget;

Heaven's gate is shut to him who comes alone;

Save thou a soul, and it shall save thy own!"

THE MEETING.

THE elder folk shook hands at last,
  Down seat by seat the signal passed.
To simple ways like ours unused,
Half solemnized and half amused,
With long-drawn breath and shrug, my guest
His sense of glad relief expressed.
Outside the hills lay warm in sun ;
The cattle in the meadow-run
Stood half-leg deep ; a single bird
The green repose above us stirred.
" What part or lot have you," he said,
" In these dull rites of drowsy-head ?
Is silence worship ? — Seek it where
It soothes with dreams the summer air,

Not in this close and rude-benched hall,

But where soft lights and shadows fall,

And all the slow, sleep-walking hours

Glide soundless over grass and flowers!

From time and place and form apart,

Its holy ground the human heart,

Nor ritual-bound nor templeward

Walks the free spirit of the Lord!

Our common Master did not pen

His followers up from other men;

His service liberty indeed,

He built no church, he framed no creed;

But while the saintly Pharisee

Made broader his phylactery,

As from the synagogue was seen

The dusty-sandalled Nazarene

Through ripening cornfields lead the way

Upon the awful Sabbath day,

His sermons were the healthful talk

That shorter made the mountain-walk,

His wayside texts were flowers and birds,

Where mingled with His gracious words

The rustle of the tamarisk-tree

And ripple-wash of Galilee."

"Thy words are well, O friend," I said ;

" Unmeasured and unlimited,

With noiseless slide of stone to stone,

The mystic Church of God has grown.

Invisible and silent stands

The temple never made with hands,

Unheard the voices still and small

Of its unseen confessional.

He needs no special place of prayer

Whose hearing ear is everywhere ;

He brings not back the childish days

That ringed the earth with stones of praise,

Roofed Karnak's hall of gods, and laid

The plinths of Philæ's colonnade.

Still less He owns the selfish good

And sickly growth of solitude, —

The worthless grace that, out of sight,

Flowers in the desert anchorite ;

Dissevered from the suffering whole,

Love hath no power to save a soul.

Not out of Self, the origin

And native air and soil of sin,

The living waters spring and flow,

The trees with leaves of healing grow.

"Dream not, O friend, because I seek

This quiet shelter twice a week,

I better deem its pine-laid floor

Than breezy hill or sea-sung shore ;

But nature is not solitude ;

She crowds us with her thronging wood ;

Her many hands reach out to us,

Her many tongues are garrulous ;

Perpetual riddles of surprise

She offers to our ears and eyes ;

She will not leave our senses still,

But drags them captive at her will ;

And, making earth too great for heaven,

She hides the Giver in the given.

"And so, I find it well to come

For deeper rest to this still room,

For here the habit of the soul,

Feels less the outer world's control ;

The strength of mutual purpose pleads

More earnestly our common needs ;

And from the silence multiplied

By these still forms on either side,

The world that time and sense have known

Falls off and leaves us God alone.

" Yet rarely through the charmed repose

Unmixed the stream of motive flows,

A flavor of its many springs,

The tints of earth and sky it brings ;

In the still waters needs must be

Some shade of human sympathy ;

And here, in its accustomed place,

I look on memory's dearest face ;

The blind by-sitter guesseth not

What shadow haunts that vacant spot ;

No eye save mine alone can see

The love wherewith it welcomes me !

And still, with those alone my kin,

In doubt and weakness, want and sin,

I bow my head, my heart I bare

As when that face was living there,

And strive (too oft, alas ! in vain)

The peace of simple trust to gain,

Fold fancy's restless wings, and lay

The idols of my heart away.

"Welcome the silence all unbroken,

Nor less the words of fitness spoken, —

Such golden words as hers for whom

Our autumn flowers have just made room ;

Whose hopeful utterance through and through

The freshness of the morning blew ;

Who loved not less the earth that light

Fell on it from the heavens in sight,

But saw in all fair forms more fair

The Eternal beauty mirrored there.

Whose eighty years but added grace

And saintlier meaning to her face, —

The look of one who bore away

Glad tidings from the hills of day,

While all our hearts went forth to meet

The coming of her beautiful feet!

Or haply hers, whose pilgrim tread

Is in the paths where Jesus led;

Who dreams her childhood's sabbath dream

By Jordan's willow-shaded stream,

And, of the hymns of hope and faith,

Sung by the monks of Nazareth,

Hears pious echoes, in the call

To prayer, from Moslem minarets fall,

Repeating where His works were wrought

The lesson that her Master taught,

Of whom an elder Sibyl gave,

The prophecies of Cumæ's cave!

"I ask no organ's soulless breath

To drone the themes of life and death,

No altar candle-lit by day,

No ornate wordsman's rhetoric-play,

No cool philosophy to teach

Its bland audacities of speech

To double-tasked idolators

Themselves their gods and worshippers,

No pulpit hammered by the fist

Of loud-asserting dogmatist,

Who borrows for the hand of love

The smoking thunderbolts of Jove.

I know how well the fathers taught,

What work the later schoolmen wrought;

I reverence old-time faith and men,

But God is near us now as then;

His force of love is still unspent,

His hate of sin as imminent;

And still the measure of our needs
Outgrows the cramping bounds of creeds;
The manna gathered yesterday
Already savors of decay;
Doubts to the world's child-heart unknown
Question us now from star and stone;
Too little or too much we know,
And sight is swift and faith is slow;
The power is lost to self-deceive
With shallow forms of make-believe.
We walk at high noon, and the bells
Call to a thousand oracles,
But the sound deafens, and the light
Is stronger than our dazzled sight;
The letters of the sacred Book
Glimmer and swim beneath our look;
Still struggles in the Age's breast
With deepening agony of quest

The old entreaty : ' Art thou He,

Or look we for the Christ to be ? '

" God should be most where man is least ;

So, where is neither church nor priest,

And never rag of form or creed

To clothe the nakedness of need, —

Where farmer-folk in silence meet, —

I turn my bell-unsummoned feet ;

I lay the critic's glass aside,

I tread upon my lettered pride,

And, lowest-seated, testify

To the oneness of humanity ;

Confess the universal want,

And share whatever heaven may grant.

He findeth not who seeks his own,

The soul is lost that 's saved alone.

Not on one favored forehead fell

4

Of old the fire-tongued miracle,

But flamed o'er all the thronging host

The baptism of the Holy Ghost;

Heart answers heart; in one desire

The blending lines of prayer aspire;

'Where, in my name, meet two or three,'

Our Lord hath said, 'I there will be!'

"So sometimes comes to soul and sense

The feeling which is evidence

That very near about us lies

The realm of spiritual mysteries.

The sphere of the supernal powers

Impinges on this world of ours.

The low and dark horizon lifts,

To light the scenic terror shifts;

The breath of a diviner air

Blows down the answer of a prayer: —

That all our sorrow, pain, and doubt

A great compassion clasps about,

And law and goodness, love and force,

Are wedded fast beyond divorce.

Then duty leaves to love its task,

The beggar Self forgets to ask ;

With smile of trust and folded hands,

The passive soul in waiting stands

To feel, as flowers the sun and dew,

The One true Life its own renew.

" So, to the calmly gathered thought

The innermost of truth is taught,

The mystery dimly understood,

That love of God is love of good,

And, chiefly, its divinest trace

In Him of Nazareth's holy face ;

That to be saved is only this, —

Salvation from our selfishness,

From more than elemental fire,

The soul's unsanctified desire,

From sin itself, and not the pain

That warns us of its chafing chain ;

That worship's deeper meaning lies

In mercy, and not sacrifice,

Not proud humilities of sense

And posturing of penitence,

But love's unforced obedience ;

That Book and Church and Day are given

For man, not God, — for earth, not heaven, —

The blessed means to holiest ends,

Not masters, but benignant friends ;

That the dear Christ dwells not afar

The king of some remoter star,

Listening, at times, with flattered ear

To homage wrung from selfish fear,

But here, amidst the poor and blind,
The bound and suffering of our kind,
In works we do, in prayers we pray,
Life of our life, he lives to-day."

THE ANSWER.

SPARE me, dread angel of reproof,
  And let the sunshine weave to-day
Its gold-threads in the warp and woof
  Of life so poor and gray.

Spare me awhile ; the flesh is weak.
  These lingering feet, that fain would stray
Among the flowers, shall some day seek
  The strait and narrow way.

Take off thy ever-watchful eye,
  The awe of thy rebuking frown ;
The dullest slave at times must sigh
  To fling his burdens down ;

To drop his galley's straining oar,

    And press, in summer warmth and calm,

The lap of some enchanted shore

    Of blossom and of balm.

Grudge not my life its hour of bloom,

    My heart its taste of long desire ;

This day be mine : be those to come

    As duty shall require.

The deep voice answered to my own,

    Smiting my selfish prayers away :

"To-morrow is with God alone,

    And man hath but to-day.

" Say not, thy fond, vain heart within,

    The Father's arms shall still be wide,

When from these pleasant ways of sin

    Thou turn'st at eventide.

"'Cast thyself down,' the tempter saith,

 'And angels shall thy feet upbear.'

He bids thee make a lie of faith,

 And blasphemy of prayer.

"Though God be good and free be Heaven,

 No force divine can love compel;

And, though the song of sins forgiven

 May sound through lowest hell,

"The sweet persuasion of His voice

 Respects thy sanctity of will.

He giveth day: thou hast thy choice

 To walk in darkness still;   ·

"As one who, turning from the light,

 Watches his own gray shadow fall,

Doubting upon his path of night,

 If there be day at all!

"No word of doom may shut thee out,

   No wind of wrath may downward whirl,

No swords of fire keep watch about

   The open gates of pearl ;

"A tenderer light than moon or sun,

   Than song of earth a sweeter hymn,

May shine and sound forever on,

   And thou be deaf and dim.

"Forever round the Mercy-seat

   The guiding lights of Love shall burn ;

But what if, habit-bound, thy feet

   Shall lack the will to turn ?

"What if thine eye refuse to see,

   Thine ear of Heaven's free welcome fail,

And thou a willing captive be,

   Thyself thy own dark jail ?

4   F

"O doom beyond the saddest guess,

    As the long years of God unroll

To make thy dreary selfishness

    The prison of a soul !

"To doubt the love that fain would break

    The fetters from thy self-bound limb ;

And dream that God can thee forsake

    As thou forsakest him !"

G. L. S.

HE has done the work of a true man, —
  Crown him, honor him, love him.
Weep over him, tears of woman,
  Stoop manliest brows above him!

O dusky mothers and daughters,
  Vigils of mourning keep for him!
Up in the mountains, and down by the waters,
  Lift up your voices and weep for him!

For the warmest of hearts is frozen,
  The freest of hands is still;
And the gap in our picked and chosen
  The long years may not fill.

No duty could overtask him,

    No need his will outrun ;

Or ever our lips could ask him,

    His hands the work had done.

He forgot his own soul for others,

    Himself to his neighbor lending ;

He found the Lord in his suffering brothers,

    And not in the clouds descending.

So the bed was sweet to die on,

    Whence he saw the doors wide swung

Against whose bolted iron

    The strength of his life was flung.

And he saw ere his eye was darkened

    The sheaves of the harvest-bringing,

And knew while his ear yet hearkened

    The voice of the reapers singing.

Ah, well! — The world is discreet ;

   There are plenty to pause and wait ;

But here was a man who set his feet

   Sometimes in advance of fate, —

Plucked off the old bark when the inner

   Was slow to renew it,

And put to the Lord's work the sinner

   When saints failed to do it.

Never rode to the wrong's redressing

   A worthier paladin.

Shall he not hear the blessing,

   "Good and faithful, enter in !"

FREEDOM IN BRAZIL.

WITH clearer light, Cross of the South, shine
    forth
  In blue Brazilian skies ;
And thou, O river, cleaving half the earth
  From sunset to sunrise,
From the great mountains to the Atlantic waves
  Thy joy's long anthem pour.
Yet a few days (God make them less !) and slaves
  Shall shame thy pride no more.
No fettered feet thy shaded margins press ;
  But all men shall walk free
Where thou, the high-priest of the wilderness,
  Hast wedded sea to sea.

And thou, great-hearted ruler, through whose mouth
  The word of God is said,
Once more, " Let there be light ! " — Son of the
    South,
  Lift up thy honored head,
Wear unashamed a crown by thy desert
  More than by birth thy own,
Careless of watch and ward ; thou art begirt
  By grateful hearts alone.   '
The moated wall and battle-ship may fail,
  But safe shall justice prove ;
Stronger than greaves of brass or iron mail
  The panoply of love.

Crowned doubly by man's blessing and God's grace,
  Thy future is secure ;
Who frees a people makes his statue's place
  In Time's Valhalla sure.

Lo! from his Neva's banks the Scythian Czar
   Stretches to thee his hand
Who, with the pencil of the Northern star,
   Wrote freedom on his land.
And he whose grave is holy by our calm
   And prairied Sangamon,
From his gaunt hand shall drop the martyr's palm
   To greet thee with "Well done!"

And thou, O Earth, with smiles thy face make
   sweet,
   And let thy wail be stilled,
To hear the Muse of prophecy repeat
   Her promise half fulfilled.
The Voice that spake at Nazareth speaks still,
   No sound thereof hath died;
Alike thy hope and heaven's eternal will
   Shall yet be satisfied.

The years are slow, the vision tarrieth long,

    And far the end may be ;

But, one by one, the fiends of ancient wrong

    Go out and leave thee free.

DIVINE COMPASSION.

L ONG since, a dream of heaven I had,
   And still the vision haunts me oft ;
I see the saints in white robes clad,
   The martyrs with their palms aloft ;
But hearing still, in middle song,
   The ceaseless dissonance of wrong ;
And shrinking, with hid faces, from the strain
Of sad, beseeching eyes, full of remorse and pain.

The glad song falters to a wail,
   The harping sinks to low lament ;
Before the still unlifted veil
   I see the crownéd foreheads bent,

Making more sweet the heavenly air,

   With breathings of unselfish prayer;

And a Voice saith : " O Pity which is pain,

O Love that weeps, fill up my sufferings which

     remain !

"Shall souls redeemed by me refuse

   To share my sorrow in their turn?

Or, sin-forgiven, my gift abuse

   Of peace with selfish unconcern ?

Has saintly ease no pitying care ?

   Has faith no work, and love no prayer?

While sin remains, and souls in darkness,

Can heaven itself be heaven, and look unmoved

     on hell ? "

Then through the Gates of Pain, I dream,

   A wind of heaven blows coolly in ;

Fainter the awful discords seem,

    The smoke of torment grows more thin,

Tears quench the burning soil, and thence

    Spring sweet, pale flowers of penitence ;

And through the dreary realm of man's despair,

Star-crowned an angel walks, and lo ! God's hope

    is there !

Is it a dream ? Is heaven so high

    That pity cannot breathe its air ?

Its happy eyes forever dry,

    Its holy lips without a prayer !

My God ! my God ! if thither led

    By thy free grace unmerited,

No crown nor palm be mine, but let me keep

A heart that still can feel, and eyes that still

    can weep.

LINES ON A FLY-LEAF.

I NEED not ask thee, for my sake,
To read a book which well may make
Its way by native force of wit
Without my manual sign to it.
Its piquant writer needs from me
No gravely masculine guaranty,
And well might laugh her merriest laugh
At broken spears in her behalf ;
Yet, spite of all the critics tell,
I frankly own I like her well.
It may be that she wields a pen
Too sharply nibbed for thin-skinned men,
That her keen arrows search and try
The armor joints of dignity,

And, though alone for error meant,

Sing through the air irreverent.

I blame her not, the young athlete

Who plants her woman's tiny feet,

And dares the chances of debate

Where bearded men might hesitate,

Who, deeply earnest, seeing well

The ludicrous and laughable,

Mingling in eloquent excess

Her anger and her tenderness,

And, chiding with a half-caress,

Strives, less for her own sex than ours,

With principalities and powers,

And points us upward to the clear

Sunned heights of her new atmosphere.

Heaven mend her faults!—I will not pause

To weigh and doubt and peck at flaws,

Or waste my pity when some fool

Provokes her measureless ridicule.

Strong-minded is she? Better so

Than dulness set for sale or show,

A household folly capped and belled

In fashion's dance of puppets held,

Or poor pretence of womanhood,

Whose formal, flavorless platitude

Is warranted from all offence

Of robust meaning's violence.

Give me the wine of thought whose bead

Sparkles along the page I read,

Electric words in which I find

The tonic of the northwest wind, —

The wisdom which itself allies

To sweet and pure humanities,

Where scorn of meanness, hate of wrong,

Are underlaid by love as strong;

The genial play of mirth that lights

Grave themes of thought, as, when on nights

Of summer-time, the harmless blaze

Of thunderless heat-lightning plays,

And tree and hill-top resting dim

And doubtful on the sky's vague rim,

Touched by that soft and lambent gleam,

Start sharply outlined from their dream.

Talk not to me of woman's sphere,

Nor point with scripture texts a sneer,

Nor wrong the manliest saint of all

By doubt, if he were here, that Paul

Would own the heroines who have lent

Grace to truth's stern arbitrament,

Foregone the praise to woman sweet,

And cast their crowns at Duty's feet;

Like her, who by her strong Appeal

Made Fashion weep and Mammon feel,

Who, earliest summoned to withstand

The color-madness of the land,

Counted her life-long losses gain,

And made her own her sisters' pain ;

Or her, who in her greenwood shade,

Heard the sharp call that Freedom made,

And, answering, struck from Sappho's lyre

Of love the Tyrtæan carmen's fire ;

Or that young girl, — Domrémy's maid

Revived a nobler cause to aid, —

Shaking from warning finger-tips

The doom of her apocalypse ;

Or her, who world-wide entrance gave

To the log-cabin of the slave,

Made all his want and sorrow known,

And all earth's languages his own.

H Y M N

FOR THE HOUSE OF WORSHIP AT GEORGETOWN,

ERECTED IN MEMORY OF A MOTHER.

THOU dwellest not, O Lord of all!
　In temples which thy children raise ;
Our work to thine is mean and small,
　And brief to thy eternal days.

Forgive the weakness and the pride,
　If marred thereby our gift may be,
For love, at least, has sanctified
　The altar that we rear to thee.

The heart and not the hand has wrought
　From sunken base to tower above

The image of a tender thought,

The memory of a deathless love !

And though should never sound of speech

Or organ echo from its wall,

Its stones would pious lessons teach,

Its shade in benedictions fall.

Here should the dove of peace be found,

And blessings and not curses given ;

Nor strife profane, nor hatred wound,

The mingled loves of earth and heaven.

Thou, who didst soothe with dying breath

The dear one watching by thy cross,

Forgetful of the pains of death

In sorrow for her mighty loss,

In memory of that tender claim,

O Mother-born, the offering take,

And make it worthy of thy name,

And bless it for a mother's sake !

THE END.

Cambridge : Electrotyped and Printed by Welch, Bigelow, & Co.

JOHN G. WHITTIER'S WRITINGS

PUBLISHED BY

FIELDS, OSGOOD, & CO., BOSTON,

And for sale by all booksellers, or sent, *post-paid*, by the Publishers
on receipt of price.

POETICAL WORKS. With Portrait. *Cabinet Edition.* 2 vols.
$ 4.00.

POETICAL WORKS. With Portrait. *Blue and Gold Edition.*
2 vols. $ 3.00.

POETICAL WORKS. Red-Line Edition. With 12 full-page Illustrations. 1 vol. Small 4to. Full gilt. $ 4.50.

POETICAL WORKS. Diamond Edition. 1 vol. $ 1.50.

AMONG THE HILLS, and other Poems. With 3 Illustrations.
1 vol. $ 1.50.

TENT ON THE BEACH, and other Poems. 1 vol. $ 1.50.

SNOW-BOUND. A Winter Idyl. A new Poem. With Portrait,
and 3 Illustrations on Wood. 1 vol. $ 1.25.

SNOW-BOUND. Illustrated Edition. With 40 Illustrations by
HARRY FENN, engraved by A. V. S. ANTHONY and W. J. LINTON. 8vo.
Cloth, full gilt, $ 5.00.

IN WAR-TIME, and other Poems. 1 vol. $ 1.25.

NATIONAL LYRICS. Illustrated. 1 vol. Paper, 50 cts ; Morocco cloth, with Portrait, $ 1.00.

HOME BALLADS AND POEMS. 1 vol. $ 1.00.

PROSE WORKS. New and Complete Edition. 2 vols. Bevelled
boards, gilt top. $ 5.00.

MAUD MULLER. Illustrated Edition. With 13 Pictures by
W. J. HENNESSY. 1 vol. Cloth, full gilt. $ 3.50.

☞ For a fuller description of the Illustrated Volumes see fol-
lowing pages.

1

THE ILLUSTRATED SNOW-BOUND.

WHITTIER'S SNOW-BOUND. With 40 Pictures by HARRY FENN, engraved by ANTHONY and LINTON. 1 vol. 8vo. Tinted paper, gilt edges, and bevelled boards, with ornamental cover. Price, in Morocco Cloth, $5.00; Turkey Morocco, $9.00.

"The well-curb had a Chinese roof;
And even the long sweep high aloof
In its slant splendor seemed to tell
Of Pisa's leaning miracle."

Of the illustrations to this exquisite Winter Idyl Mr. Whittier says: "It gives me pleasure to commend the illustrations which accompany this edition of 'Snow-Bound,' for the faithfulness with which they present the spirit and the details of the passages and places that the artist has designed them to accompany."

"The illustrations and the poem fit together so perfectly, forming a beautiful and harmonious whole, that one can hardly be said to have read 'Snow-Bound' unless he has read it in this edition." — *New York Times.*

MAUD MULLER ILLUSTRATED.

WHITTIER'S MAUD MULLER. With 13 Illustrations drawn by W. J. HENNESSY, and engraved by A. V. S. ANTHONY and others.

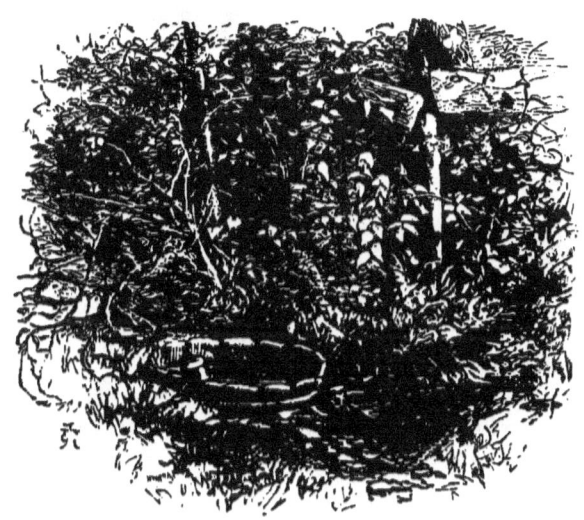

This edition of one of the most charming and popular ballads in our language is beautifully illustrated, elegantly printed on thick tinted paper, and bound in handsome morocco cloth with bevelled boards and gilt edges.

Price, 8vo, Cloth, gilt, $3.50; Morocco Antique, $7.00.

WHITTIER'S NATIONAL LYRICS.

With Illustrations by various Artists. A charming Pocket Edition of WHITTIER'S most popular patriotic poems. Bound in Morocco Cloth, with Portrait. Price, $1.00.

3

THE RED-LINE WHITTIER.

Illustrated with 12 full-page Pictures by various Artists.

KATHLEEN.

This first and only complete Illustrated Edition of WHITTIER ever published contains all of MR. WHITTIER's hitherto published Poems, is handsomely printed on fine tinted paper, each page bordered with a red-ruled line, and is illustrated with 12 engravings by the best artists. It is a small quarto, uniform with the "Red-Line TENNYSON."

Price, in Cloth, $4.50; Half Calf, $6.00; Morocco, $8.00.

4